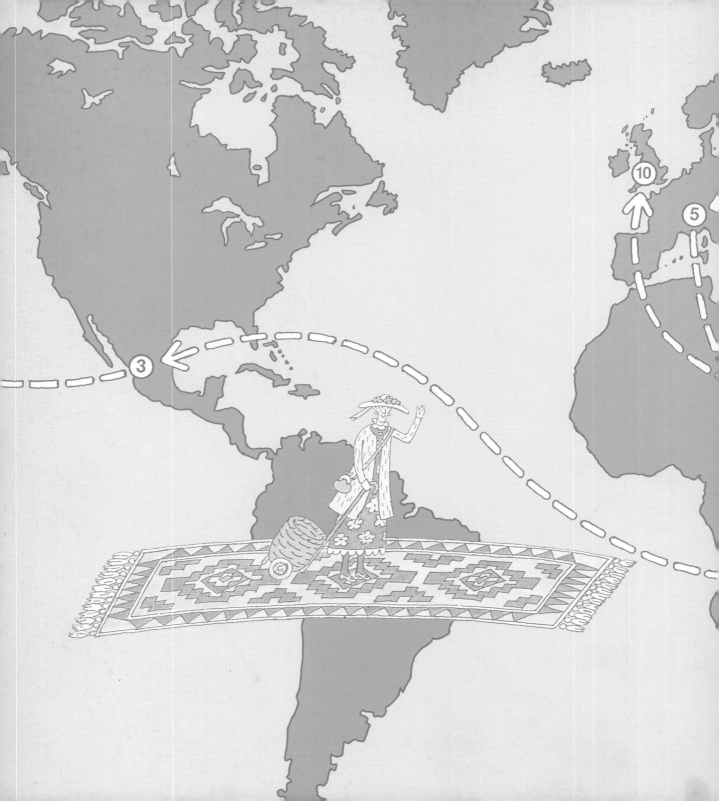

My Granny went to Market

BAREFOOT BEGINNERS
an imprint of
Barefoot Books Ltd
PO Box 95 Kingswood Bristol BS30 5BH

This book has been printed on 100% acid-free paper

Graphic design: Design/Section
Printed in Singapore by Tien Wah Press Pte Ltd
Paperback ISBN 1 901223 43 4

3 5 7 9 8 6 4 2

My Granny went to Market

A Round-the-World Counting Rhyme

words by Stella Blackstone *pictures by* Bernard Lodge

BAREFOOT BOOKS

BATH

My granny went to market
to buy a flying carpet.

She bought the flying carpet
from a man in Istanbul,
it was trimmed with yellow tassels
and made of knotted wool.

Next she went to Thailand
and flew down from the sky
to buy herself two temple cats,
Puyin and Puchai.*

*'Puyin' means little girl
'Puchai' means little boy

Then she headed westwards
to the land of Mexico;
she bought three fierce and funny masks,
one red, one blue, one yellow.

The flying carpet seemed to know
exactly where to take her;
they went to China next, to buy
four lanterns made of paper.*

* the symbol on the lanterns means
'double happiness'.

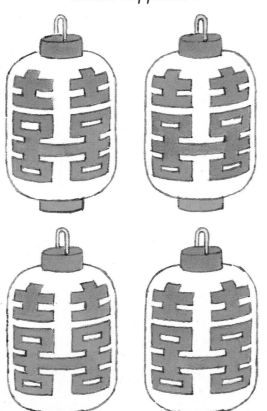

'To Switzerland!' cried Granny
as the carpet turned around,
she bought five cowbells there, that made
a funny clanking sound.

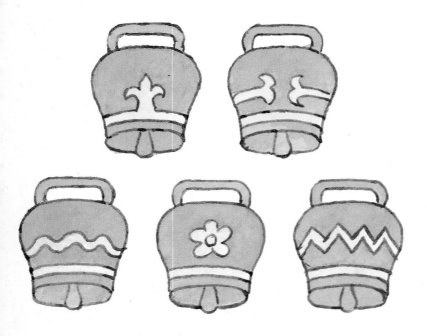

'Now Africa!' sang Granny,
'We must wake the morning sun!'
So they spiralled south to Kenya
where she bought six booming drums.

Next they travelled northwards,
past the homes of mountain trolls,
to stop awhile in Russia
for seven nesting dolls.

'Australia!' Granny ordered,
'Take me down to Alice Springs.
I want eight buzzing boomerangs
that fly back without wings.'

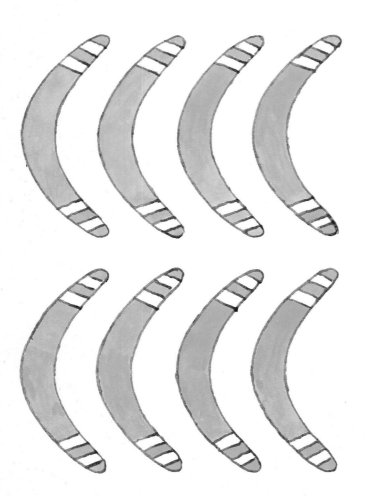

Then Granny sighed 'I've bought so much,
but nothing Japanese!'
In Tokyo she found nine kites
that fluttered in the breeze.

But best of all, she came back home
down Canterbury Lane,
where she bought me a black pony
with ten ribbons in his mane.

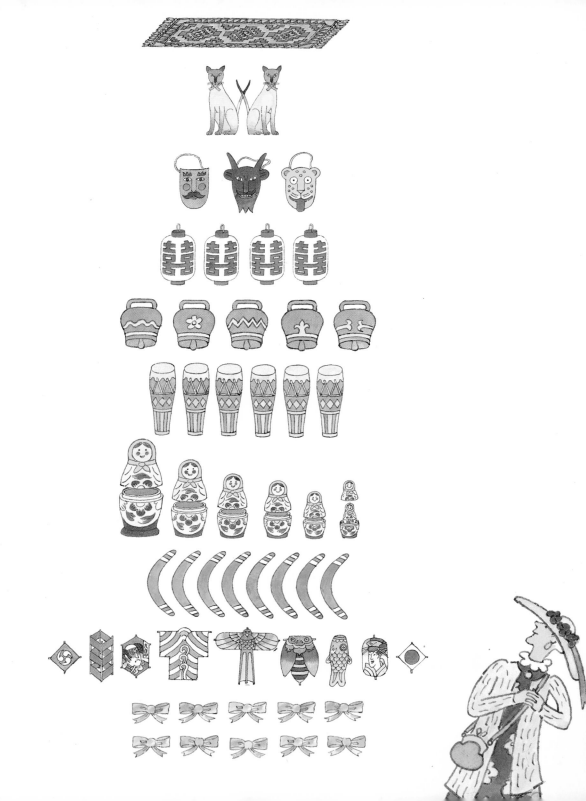

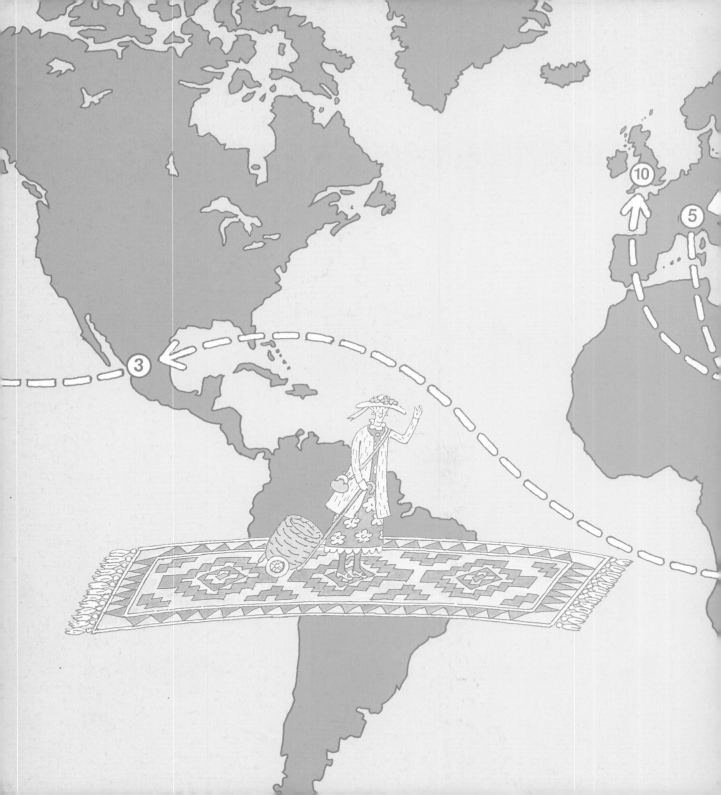

BAREFOOT BOOKS publishes high-quality picture books for children of all ages and specialises in the work of artists and writers from many cultures. If you have enjoyed this book and would like to receive a copy of our current catalogue, please contact our London office – tel: 0171 704 6492 fax: 0171 359 5798   email: sales@barefoot-books.com website: www.barefoot-books.com